ELEPHANT LEARNS TO SHARE

A book about SHARING

Written by Sue Graves

Illustrated by Trevor Dunton

W
FRANKLIN WATTS
LONDON·SYDNEY

Elephant was very selfish. He would not share **anything**. He would not share his sweets.

He would not share his toys.

He would not even share his games. He always kept **everything** for himself.

At school, he would not share his paints, even when Monkey ran out of yellow paint and could not finish his picture. Elephant said the paints were **his** and he **did not want** to share them. Monkey thought he was mean.

At break, he would not share his snack,
even when Hippo forgot to bring his own
snack to school. Elephant said he wanted
his snack **for himself**. Hippo thought he
was very mean.

On Friday, Elephant was really selfish. He would not share any of the books in the library corner. Little Lion said Elephant **did not need** all the books at once. He said Elephant could only read one book at a time. But Elephant said he wanted all the books for himself.

Little Lion told Miss Bird. Miss Bird said Elephant could not stay in the library corner if he did not share nicely.

At playtime, Elephant found an old football under a bush. Everyone wanted to play with it, but Elephant said **he found it** so it was **his football** and he did not have to share it if he did not want to. His friends got **cross**. They thought he was mean not to share.

11

On Saturday morning, Elephant's gran came to visit. She had a **nice surprise** for Elephant. It was a new bat and ball set. It had a shiny red ball and a big wooden bat with a bright blue handle. Elephant thought it was the best bat and ball set in the world.

First of all, Elephant threw the ball. He threw it really hard. It went a long, long way.

Then Elephant swung the bat. It swung really well. Elephant was very pleased.

Next, Elephant tried to throw
the ball... **and bat it**.
But it was no good.

Then he tried to bat the ball...
and catch it. But that was
no good either.

Elephant was **not pleased**.
His new bat and ball set was
no fun at all.

Elephant went off to find his friends. They were by the swamp. They were playing with an old bat and ball set. The ball was not shiny at all and the bat's handle was bent and broken – but everyone was having lots of fun.

Elephant told his friends about his new bat and ball set. He told them about the shiny red ball and the big wooden bat with the bright blue handle, but no one was interested. They were having too much fun **playing together** with the old bat and ball set.

Then Elephant asked if he could play, too. But everyone said **no**. They said he did not share with them **ever**! So they did not want to share their game with him. Elephant went home. He felt very sad.

Elephant saw Gran in the garden. She asked him why he was sad. He told her that his friends did not want to share with him because he had never shared with them. He said he wished he could **put things right**. Gran told him to think about how he could do that.

Elephant had a good think. He said he should say **sorry** to his friends for being so **selfish**. He said he should **ask** his friends to come and play with his new bat and ball set. Gran said that they were good ideas.

Elephant found his friends. He said he was **sorry** for not sharing with them. He promised never to be selfish again. Then he asked them if they would like to come and play bat and ball at his house. Everyone said **yes**.

23

Everyone liked Elephant's new bat and ball set. They liked the shiny red ball and the big wooden bat with the bright blue handle.

Elephant let everyone **take turns** at swinging the bat.

He let everyone **take turns** at throwing the ball.

Next, they all played a game **together**.
Everyone said it was the best game ever.
Elephant was pleased.

Soon it was time for tea. Gran had made a large cake with lots of cherries on the top. It looked delicious. Elephant cut the cake into slices. He made sure everyone had a **fair share**. He made sure everyone had a cherry, too. He said it was **nicer to share things** with your friends…
and much **more fun**!
Everyone agreed!

A note about sharing this book

The *Behaviour Matters* series has been developed to provide a starting point for further discussion on children's behaviour, both in relation to themselves and others. The series is set in the jungle with animal characters reflecting typical behaviour traits often seen in young children.

Elephant Learns to Share

This story explores the problems that can occur when children do not share with others and the isolation and loneliness that can follow.

The book aims to encourage children to develop ways of engaging with their peers. It highlights the point that to share is preferable to being lonely and suggests ways in which a child might engage with others.

How to use the book

The book is designed for adults to share with either an individual child or a group of children, and as a starting point for discussion.

The book also provides visual support and repeated words and phrases to build reading confidence.

Before reading the story

Choose a time to read when you and the children are relaxed and have time to share the story.

Spend time looking at the illustrations and talk about what the book might be about before reading it together.

Encourage children to employ a phonics first approach to tackling new words by sounding the words out.

After reading, talk about the book with the children:

- What was the story about? Have the children ever wanted to keep all their toys for themselves? Have they ever resented having to share with brothers, sisters or friends in class? Encourage them to explain why they were reluctant to share with others. Ask them if playing alone was as much fun as playing with a friend or sibling.

- Extend this by asking the children if anyone has ever refused to share with them. How did they feel? Did they feel angry or upset? Did they think the other person was selfish? Did they also resist sharing with this person because of their behaviour?

- Talk about the benefits of sharing with others. Some games for example would be impossible to play unless others took part. Invite the children to think of games and activities that they have especially enjoyed with their friends.

- Take the opportunity to talk about coping with someone who doesn't want to share. How could they help someone who doesn't share? Point out that the best way to encourage others to share is to lead by example.

- Talk about the importance of saying 'sorry' to those who have been upset. Explain how this can make the person feel better if someone has refused to share with them.

- Invite children to role-play the parts of Elephant and his friends in the story using the strategies for encouraging Elephant to share that have been discussed earlier.

- Encourage the children in groups to co-operate on an activity, for example making a model. Encourage them to share resources and to ensure that each member of the group is allowed to contribute fully.

Franklin Watts
First published in Great Britain in 2015 by The Watts Publishing Group

Series Editor: Jackie Hamley
Series Designer: Cathryn Gilbert

A CIP catalogue record for this book is available
from the British Library.

ISBN 978 1 4451 4245 6 (hbk)
ISBN 978 1 4451 4246 3 (library ebook)

Printed in China

Franklin Watts
An imprint of
Hachette Children's Group
Part of The Watts Publishing Group
Carmelite House
50 Victoria Embankment
London EC4Y 0DZ

An Hachette UK Company
www.hachette.co.uk

www.franklinwatts.co.uk